Breath of the Dragon

Breath of the Dragon

by Gail Giles
Illustrated by June Otani

Clarion Books ～ New York

Thanks to Kim Vacher-Ta for her help with the pronunciation
and definition of Thai words.

Clarion Books
a Houghton Mifflin Company imprint
215 Park Avenue South, New York, NY 10003
Text copyright © 1997 by Gail Giles
Illustrations copyright © 1997 by June Otani

The illustrations for this book were executed in pen, ink, wash,
and watercolor on Arches hot press paper.
The text is set in 13/18.5-point Caslon.

For information about this and other Houghton Mifflin trade and reference books and
multimedia products, visit The Bookstore at Houghton Mifflin on the World Wide Web at
(http://www.hmco.com/trade/).

Printed in the USA

Library of Congress Cataloging-in-Publication Data

Giles, Gail.
Breath of the dragon / by Gail Giles
p. cm.
Summary: Malila draws pictures to accompany her grandmother's stories
about Thai festivals, traditions, and customs.
ISBN 0-395-76476-9
[1. Thailand–Social life and customs–Fiction.   2. Grandmothers–Fiction.
3. Artists–Fiction.]   I. Title.
PZ7.G3923Br   1997
[Fic]–dc20   96-42067
CIP
AC

VB   10   9   8   7   6   5   4   3   2   1

To Jim Giles
and
Josh Jakubik,
whose presence enriches my world,
and
to the memory of
Angelo Orsini,
Donna Clement,
and Jeanette Nelson,
whose absence diminishes it.
–G. G.

For Jennifer Baluyut
–J. O.

Chapter One~

ON A QUIET AND STAR-FILLED NIGHT in a village near
Bangkok, Malila's father came to kiss her good night.

"Good night, Malila Noi, my small flower," he murmured as he pulled the cover up to her chin. "May you
find magic in your sleep and your dreams be filled with
laughter."

Malila stirred as her father's light kiss awakened her.
She opened her sleep-heavy eyes just in time to see him

leaving. She smiled dreamily as her handsome father walked away into the darkness.

She never saw him again.

—

Malila woke the next morning to the sound of weeping. Why was someone crying? she wondered. It was such a fine, bright morning. Malila was five years old, and the idea that someone would weep on a sunny morning seemed silly to her.

Malila heard the tinkle of the temple bells and the cheerful calls of the vendors as they paddled their boats along the river to market. Rolling from her sleeping mat, she padded barefoot to the window. She was too short to see out of the window, but she loved to play with the shafts of sunlight that streamed through the slatted bamboo blinds.

Malila stood on her tiptoes and stretched her hands toward the window. She reached forward and "touched" a beam of light with the tip of one finger, then another finger and another and another. Then she stepped into the ray of light and let the sun warm her eyes, her nose, and her cheeks.

The sound of weeping interrupted her play. *That sounds like my mother,* she thought. *Why is my mother crying?*

Malila trotted across her sleeping mat and peeked around the curtain that divided her mat from the main room. She saw her mother sitting on the floor at the low table. Her face was bent to her hands and she was sobbing.

A man wearing the dark blue uniform of a policeman was standing next to her mother, looking down and talking to her in low, gruff tones. He seemed very stern. As Malila watched silently, hidden among the folds of the curtain, Mother looked up and murmured something to the officer. She seemed afraid of him. He grunted, then turned quickly and left the house.

Malila ran to her mother and tried to wriggle into her lap. Mother waved her away, put her face back into her cupped hands, and sobbed piteously. After a time she quieted her sobs and looked across the table at Malila, sitting cross-legged and very silent.

"Malila, you must get dressed," she said in a tired voice. "We must go to your grandmother's." Then she got up and went to her own sleeping room behind the curtain.

Malila waited, unsure of what to do. When her mother did not come out to dress her, Malila went to her room and pulled out her clothes. She had never dressed herself before and she was confused. She struggled into her loose trousers, shoved her feet into her sandals, and

–3–

pulled on her blouse, but her little fingers could not make the buttons behave. She came out with only one button holding her blouse together. Mother did not notice.

She hurried Malila out of the house and into the street. The street ran along the canal and was filled with carts pulled by oxen. Malila saw their neighbors watching them hurry by. The neighbors whispered to each other and shook their heads and clucked their tongues. They looked away when Malila looked at them.

Malila and her mother arrived at a hut that Malila recognized. It belonged to her father's mother. This grandmother did not visit Malila's family often. The only time Malila had been to her home was to celebrate Grandmother's fifth-cycle birthday. Malila had been told then that to reach sixty years old was a great achievement and that they would feast with her father's mother on that day. That had been over a year ago. Malila remembered that harsh words had been exchanged and they had not visited again.

Mother knocked on the door of the hut. She and Malila took off their shoes and left them on the porch, because wearing shoes in the house would be disrespectful.

Malila heard the soft slap of slippers as her grandmother came to the door. Grandmother was small and thin, with gray hair pulled back into an old-fashioned braid. Her eyes were brown and bright and seemed surprised. She gave them a small, wistful smile and placed her palms together, fingers pointing up. With her fingertips just below her chin, she bowed her head very slightly. Malila and her mother also put their hands together in the *wai* and bowed.

Malila's grandmother gave them a polite greeting, "*Sawatdee*," and stepped aside for them to enter.

Malila's mother looked both frightened and ashamed as she gestured for Malila to sit on the porch and wait. She did not wash from the jar by the door as any guest should, and this confused Malila even more. Mother ducked her head as she passed Malila's grandmother. In Thailand, one must keep one's head lower than the head of any elder when one moves past.

Malila sat under the open window, hoping for a clue that would unravel the mystery of her morning. She could hear her mother's soft, whispering voice from inside the hut, and then she heard the sound of her grandmother weeping. The talking continued for some time, interrupted over and over again by the sound of her mother's crying.

Finally, Mother called her into the hut. "Malila," she said, "great sadness has come to us. Your father has died."

Malila did not understand what had happened, but

she knew it was something very bad. "I don't understand. What is *died*? When is my father coming home?"
Her lip trembled.

"Do you remember the time your puppy was run over
by the cart when he ran into the street? He died when
the cart hit him. The same thing happened to your
father."

"My father was run over by a cart in the street?"

Malila's mother began to cry again. "No, he wasn't
killed by a cart. But he is dead just the same. He is not
coming home again."

Malila began sobbing and flung herself into her mother's arms. Mother patted her on the back, then pulled
away. "I must go to make arrangements for the funeral.
Stay with your grandmother." She rushed out to the
porch, slipped on her shoes, and disappeared into the
crowded street.

Malila knew about funerals. She had gone to one
recently with her parents. The rite was elaborate, with
monks chanting verses from the Buddhist scriptures.
After the ceremony the mourners feasted, played chess,
and made merry to banish the sorrow from the lives of
the friends and relatives. Musicians played the timpani
and java pipes all day long.

Malila looked up at her grandmother. Tears filled her
eyes once again.

"Come, Malila." Her grandmother's voice was soft and gentle. "We must go to the spirit house. Let's pick some flowers. We need special help to keep away the evil spirits."

They went out and began picking jasmine and orchids and the small malila flower that grew along the banks of the *klong*. Malila had been named for this tiny flower. It was about the size of her thumb, purple when a closed bud, white when in bloom.

After they had filled the basket that she carried, Malila's grandmother motioned for her to follow her back into the house. When they stepped onto the porch, the old woman removed the dipper from the water jar that stood by the door. She poured the water out of the jar onto the ground, then turned the jar upside down. She took the small ladder that led to the porch and turned it upside down also, saying, "My son was a discontented spirit. His discontent will spread to us if his soul resides here. This will keep his soul from entering the house."

Malila nodded but kept silent. She did not understand what was happening. She was overwhelmed with questions and could not sort out which she should ask first. She decided to ask nothing now and wait for this old woman to explain things.

They went into the house and Grandmother pointed

at a place on the floor. Malila sat, holding the basket of flowers in her lap.

Grandmother sat near Malila, opened an enameled box, and brought out a large needle, which she threaded with thick thread. She held out her hand and nodded. Malila held up a jasmine bloom. Her grandmother smiled at her and nodded again. She took the bloom gently, pierced the stem with the needle, and pushed the flower to the end of the thread. Malila had another bloom ready. Grandmother strung the jasmine and orchids until the long thread was full, then tied the ends together, making a large circle of flowers. She tucked the purple malila buds between the bigger flowers, picked up a lotus flower, and tied it at the top of the circle.

Malila looked up at her grandmother. "My mother never made one of these."

Grandmother sighed. "My son didn't follow the traditions. We argued about this and became almost strangers." She looked down at the flowers, and Malila thought she saw a mist of tears in her grandmother's eyes.

"Once I brought a small spirit house to your hut. Is it still there?"

"No," Malila said.

"Ah," Grandmother said. "So much anger and sadness." Malila watched in silence while her grandmother wiped her eyes.

"Then I will explain," Grandmother went on. "The spirit and guardian of the house is called Chao Thi. Without his favor, we have no protection from the evil spirits. My son died without the goodwill of Chao Thi, so we must make an extra effort to please him. These flowers will please him because the lotus is a symbol of purity and perfection, and the malila is a special message from you. I think we will give him special food as well."

Malila's grandmother rose and went to the front door, and Malila followed. The front of the house faced the Chao Phraya River, with steps leading down to the water where the vendors floated by in their little market boats. Malila's grandmother watched for a moment, then called to one of the boatmen. The man, dressed in the traditional wide-brimmed straw hat and dark blue loose pants and jacket, turned his little boat and paddled to the steps of the hut.

Malila's grandmother bought a small watermelon, carried it into the kitchen, and placed it on a low table. As Malila watched, Grandmother selected a small, thin-bladed paring knife from some utensils hanging on the wall. She sat at the table and carved the melon into an intricate flower, petal by petal.

"This is finished. Now I will prepare *pla dek*. Have you had *pla dek*?"

Malila nodded. She loved the small strips of raw fish

marinated in a spicy sauce. This dish was reserved for special holidays, and her mother had not made it often.

Finally Grandmother said, "We are ready now, Malila. You must watch me and make the *wai* and the *krap* as I do."

"Yes, Grandmother," Malila said as she followed the old woman outside.

The spirit house was on a tall pole. It had a sharply pointed roof that hung over the sides and turned up at the end in a graceful curve. The roof was a bright blue, with shiny squares of tin that reflected the sun. The sides were yellow with pink and green trim.

"This is the *san phra phum*, the home of Chao Thi," Grandmother explained. "The spirit house must face north and must be far enough from the roof of the hut that no shadow ever falls upon it. The shiny parts reflect the faces of the evil spirits. When the spirits see their own faces, they are frightened away."

Malila's grandmother placed the watermelon and the *pla dek* on the platform in front of the spirit house, nodded for Malila to hand her the string of flowers, and laid this on the house itself. Next she put her palms together in the *wai*. She knelt and bowed her head to touch the ground, performing the most reverent *krap*, usually reserved for monks or royalty. She made the *wai* three

times, each time placing her hands on the ground next to her knees.

Malila knelt next to her grandmother and tried to do as she did. Somehow, the tears she had been holding back flooded her eyes and fell onto the dusty ground.

Soon Grandmother got slowly to her feet. "You must take a nap now, Malila. This has been a very difficult day for you."

"Grandmother, I have to wait for my mother. She will come back soon," Malila said.

Her grandmother sighed. "Take a nap, Malila. Sometimes things do not happen as we expect they will."

Malila knelt on the ground until her grandmother extended her wrinkled hand. Malila took it and rose. She followed the old woman into the hut.

Chapter Two~

MALILA DID NOT WAKE until the next morning. The sun streamed through the windows just as it had the day before, but Malila did not play her game with the sunbeams. This was not her house or her window, and so these were not her sunbeams. She would play the game when her mother returned and she woke in her own room again.

Malila heard a low, gruff sound, like a bark. She rubbed her eyes and saw a lizard more than a foot long

running across the floor. She scrambled from her mat and went into the main room of the house.

"Grandmother, there is a monster in that room."

"A monster?"

"Yes, it looks like a dragon and–" Malila was interrupted by a loud knocking sound.

To Malila's surprise, Grandmother smiled. "That's not a dragon. That is a barking lizard. Not every house is lucky enough to have one. He's believed to bring good fortune to the house."

"Is he making that noise?"

"Yes, he has a heavy tail and if he gets frightened he slaps it around. You must have frightened him."

Malila relaxed a bit. "Is he like a gecko? We have one at my house. He eats the mosquitoes."

"Yes, something like that. I hope you slept well."

Malila remembered yesterday. "Grandmother, where is my mother? She didn't come back for me!"

"Come to me, little one."

Malila walked slowly to her grandmother, who pulled her into her lap. Malila thought that her grandmother felt hard and bony, not soft and comforting like her mother. She didn't like it here. She wanted to go home. She wanted all of yesterday to have been a dream.

"Grandchild, your mother isn't coming back for you for a while," Grandmother told her. "She's gone to Bangkok where her eldest brother lives. He has promised to send her across the skies to America. She will send for you when she has made a fine new life."

Malila covered her ears so that she could hear no more. Her father had left her, and her mother was flying into the sky. Her whole world had changed. All the people she loved were gone. Why had they left her with an old woman she hardly knew? She felt alone and very frightened.

She remembered what her father had always told her when she was unhappy or afraid. "Never mind," he would say, "these things will change." Malila would wait, and things would change.

She uncovered her ears and eased off of Grandmother's lap. "*Mai pen rai,*" she muttered. "Never mind."

❧

Grandmother got up and went into the kitchen.

Malila followed. Her grandmother was scooping rice, steamed fish, and vegetables into a bowl.

"Come in, Malila, we can eat after the monks," she said.

Malila went to the window and saw several robed monks walking slowly down the road in a line. "I've seen monks in the street, but never so many together," she told Grandmother.

"Well," Grandmother said, "the *wat* is very close and they have just left it."

"Where are they going?" Malila asked.

"Ah, I forget what the young don't know," Grandmother said, taking the bowl of food to the door. "Let me explain. These monks come from a group of buildings called a *wat*. It holds the village school, the prayer temple, and the living place of the monks. They come to beg food. They must beg for all of their food to show that they are humble."

When the monks came near the house, one whose yellow robe and shaven head showed that he was a *bhiksu*, a full-fledged monk, separated from the others and came to Malila's grandmother's door. Without speaking, the monk placed his alms bowl on the floor in front of Grandmother. She pushed food from her bowl into the monk's. Then she bowed and thanked the monk for accepting it. The monk picked up his bowl and slid silently away.

Grandmother returned to the earthenware stove. She scooped more of the rice, fish, and vegetables from the pan into two bowls. "Since you did not keep the old ways, your mother probably did not feed the monks."

"My mother doesn't cook often. We buy things like soup and noodles from the carts and eat in the market-place, not at home."

Nodding, Grandmother said, "Many of the younger people do this now. Things change." She paused a moment, then went on. "You see, giving is good and pleases Buddha. You must not give for thanks or expect return. To feed the monk is an act of merit-making, and the monk knows he cannot thank the donor without robbing her of her merit."

Malila's grandmother put their bowls on the table and sat down. She nodded to Malila, who sat and ate her breakfast silently, following her grandmother's every movement with her eyes.

The old woman ate quickly, not speaking to Malila. The house was still. Malila could hear the crickets in the tall grasses and the murmur of the river as it hurried past the door of the hut. She picked at her food and fought back tears. She would not let anyone see her fear or her pain.

Her grandmother finished her meal. Her eyes met Malila's. "Little one," she said, "forgive an old woman who has lived alone too long. I'm not used to another person at my table."

Malila lowered her eyes. She could not hold all the tears back. One escaped her eye and rolled down her cheek.

Malila's grandmother sighed. "Come with me, Grandchild." She held out her hand.

Malila looked up. A shy, hesitant smile appeared on her grandmother's face. Slowly, Malila stretched out her hand.

Grandmother grasped Malila's plump, soft hand in her thin one that was spotted with age and callused from work. They held on to each other as they walked out to the porch.

"Sit here with me, Malila."

They sat on stools. The river rushed by the porch.

"I am unused to talking to people, Malila. My only friend for many years has been this river. He talks to me and I listen."

"The river talks?" Malila asked, puzzled.

"Yes; be very quiet and listen."

The river gurgled and swished and rumbled. The sound was gentle and soothing. Tears no longer burned Malila's eyes.

"Do you hear?"

Malila nodded.

"The river is telling me that I am an old and foolish woman. That my life has changed. My son is dead and I must accept this pain."

Malila lowered her eyes again.

"Yes, Malila, this is something you must accept too."

"But I want my daddy back."

Malila's grandmother was quiet for a long time. She patted Malila's hand.

"You must take this pain and hold it tightly so that it cannot grow. Have *jai yen*, cool heart. Learn that if you cannot change a thing, you must accept it."

Malila shook her head.

Her grandmother laughed. "The river says again that I am an old fool. It also says you should remember your grandmother's words when you are old enough to understand them."

She stood up. "The river says that the gods have sent me a gift. That I am not alone anymore. If you accept your fate the gods will send you gifts also, Malila." She held out her hand again. "Come inside with me."

Malila shook her head. "The river says I should wait here for my mother."

"She is not coming, Malila."

"The river says she is."

"And the river never lies. But it talks of a day to come. Not today. Come inside now."

"I'll wait here for my mother."

Malila's grandmother went into the hut.

Malila waited on the porch all day. She watched the river craft and the people who piloted them: the butcher in his bobbing sampan, the women who steered their vegetable boats up to the loading platforms on every porch, the coffee salesman, the girl with betel-blackened teeth who sold chilies and garlic. She watched the barges loaded with rice, the rafts of teak wood, and the tugboats that steamed and puffed toward the mills. She saw the traffic policeman in his boat, who came to untangle a clog of boats.

Finally, when the sky became dark, Malila trudged into the hut. She saw a bowl of rice and vegetables on a small table in her room. She sat down on her sleeping

mat and ate the rice slowly. It was still warm. Her grandmother's kindness made the tears she had been fighting spring into her eyes.

Malila finished her meal, set the bowl carefully on the small table, and curled up on her side. She scrubbed the tears from her cheek with her fist. Her grandmother came into the room and sat next to her.

"She didn't come," Malila said.

"I'm sorry, Malila. She'll come another day."

But the day had been long and Malila had stopped believing that her mother would come back out of the sky. She decided to hold her pain tight as Grandmother had told her.

"*Mai pen rai,*" Malila said. "I don't care, now. I don't care."

Malila's grandmother patted Malila's hand. "The river says you do, Malila. And the river never lies."

Chapter Three~

MALILA'S GRANDMOTHER WAS A DRESSMAKER. She made ornamental costumes worn by the dancers and minor members of the court for the fifteen major Thai festivals. She worked in the main room of the hut, sitting in a chair woven of straw. The floor was covered with scraps of silk and satin that were all the colors of the rainbow.

Malila sat on a mat and watched her grandmother

sew. The silver needle flashed and the shiny scissors snipped and the thread stitched magic into the cloth. Her grandmother talked as she worked. She told Malila about her own father, who had been a rice farmer. She told her about riding the water buffalo with her younger brother. She told Malila about her husband, who had been in the military, and cousins who were in the military now. She told her about choosing colors and fabrics for the costumes.

Sometimes, Malila would watch the river from the window. She would pick out a sampan and watch until it disappeared around the curve of the river. Even though Malila could tell that her grandmother was watching her and waiting for an answer or a question, she rarely spoke.

Three days passed, one much like the next. On the fourth day, Malila noticed something different. There was a doll lying next to her grandmother's enameled sewing box.

Malila looked at the doll and then at her grandmother. She wondered why an old woman would need a doll. Could this doll be meant for Malila? She stretched out her hand toward the doll but pulled back before touching it. No, surely not. This doll could not be meant for her. She shrugged and folded her hands in her lap.

Her grandmother began threading the silver needle. "It is only a poor homemade doll," she said.

"It's a pretty doll," Malila said. Maybe it *was* for her.

"Well, it has long black hair of embroidery floss. It looks a bit like you, I think."

She was meant to have this doll! Malila reached out and pulled the doll into her lap. "Oh no," Malila said. "I think it is a princess doll."

"Well, I don't know. She doesn't have any clothes. It is just a stuffed doll. Not a princess at all."

"Oh yes," said Malila. "She is a princess. If she had fine clothes, you would see."

"Maybe so. Maybe this princess doll could have clothes made from these scraps."

Malila nodded. She reached for a scrap of green silk, shot through with gold threads. "This is a good piece," she said. "Someone would love her if she wore this."

In the days that followed, Malila played with the doll that her grandmother had made for her. She dressed the doll with scraps of the brocades, satins, and cloudlike silks that her grandmother used for costumes. Her grandmother sang to Malila as she worked. Soon Malila hummed along with Grandmother, then sang with her.

Grandmother began telling stories about the beautiful dancers and the lords and ladies of the courts who would wear the costumes. She sometimes left a story unfinished and Malila would ask to hear the ending.

"I'm not sure I remember. How do you think it should end?" Grandmother would ask.

Malila gave all the stories happy endings.

For Malila's sixth birthday, Grandmother gave her some colored chalks. Malila drew pictures of princesses and ladies of the court.

"Malila," her grandmother would say, "draw a picture of the princess in a blue dress. A dress of soft silk for dancing.

"Now, draw a red dress for the *fawn lep*. This is a beautiful dance, and the red dresses are supposed to make the dancers look like orchids."

Malila drew a dress with layers that looked like petals of a flower.

"Draw a dress for a wedding. Something grand. Make sure it has many jewels." Malila drew a flowing gown that dazzled with diamonds and a headpiece thick with sapphires and emeralds.

"Once long ago there was a king named Rama," Grandmother said. "When he died he left two sons. One son was Mongkut, and he was the rightful heir to the throne.

"Late one night, one of the court dancers came to Mongkut's window and called to him. She told Mongkut that his half brother had plans to assassinate him that very night. The court dancer said she had overheard the plans being made when she was changing her costume during the performance that night. She told Mongkut that she had brought him a monk's saffron robe and a begging bowl. She also had a boat ready for him. He would have to steal away in the night disguised as a monk in order to save his life. He did this and lived many years as a monk before he regained his rightful place as king.

"Draw a picture of the court dancer handing Mongkut the monk's robes."

Malila loved her grandmother's stories of things gone wrong and then put right in the end. She eagerly drew pictures to go with them.

Now she was happy in her grandmother's thatched-roof house on the bank of the *klong*. But she still waited for her mother to come back for her.

Malila's grandmother taught her the old ways of the Thai people. "People will watch you carefully, trying to prove that you were not brought up properly. You must avoid all the taboos. You must never peer over another's head. If you pass an elder, you must keep your head below his. If he is sitting, you must crawl rather than insult his personal spirit.

"You must never point at another with a foot. It is the lowliest part of the body. You must never cross your legs when you speak with another person. You must sit with your feet tucked under you when you sit on the floor. If you sit in a chair, both feet must rest on the floor. Most important, you must learn to behave with *krengjai*, consideration. You must always be polite and humble; show respect and obedience."

They ate the traditional Thai foods. Malila loved *nam pla*, an amber-colored fish sauce made with garlic and chili, as well as another sauce made of dried, salted shrimps pounded with sugar, garlic, and lime juice. Her grandmother made many different curries, sweet, sour, bitter, and peppery. Malila liked *haum*, a spicy pork sausage, and shark fin and bird's nest soup. All of this was new to her. The food she knew best was the noodles and rice and vegetable dishes her mother bought from street vendors. Still, her favorite dish was one her mother had made. It was a dessert, rich coconut milk made into a pudding and wrapped in banana leaves. Her grandmother ate with her fingers in the old way, but gave Malila a fork and spoon and taught her to use them.

One day a mailman came to the door. He handed Malila's grandmother a white envelope. They rarely got mail, and Malila was curious. Her grandmother took the white square to the low dining table and set it down. She and Malila sat, feet tucked under them on the floor, and looked at it.

"This writing looks very strange," Malila said, pointing at the return address.

"Those are words in English. This is from your mother."

Malila's heart leaped, but she kept her face still. Things might not happen as she wanted them to. "Open it, Grandmother," she said quietly.

Malila's grandmother read slowly, then folded the thin sheet of paper and put it back into the envelope.

"Is she coming for me now? She has been gone long enough to make a good life, I think." Malila's voice quavered, and she felt as if she had swallowed a live fish.

"Making a good life can take a long time," Malila's grandmother said. "Your mother says that America is strange to her and she finds learning the language very difficult. She is afraid and lonely."

"If she sent for me, she wouldn't be so lonely."

Malila's grandmother put one crooked finger under Malila's chin and lifted her face. "I think that your mother does not want to escape from a tiger only to meet a crocodile."

"I don't understand."

Malila thought her grandmother's brown eyes looked like the river–wise, but dark and clouded. "Maybe your mother doesn't want you to be afraid and lonely as she is," Grandmother said.

"Or maybe she just doesn't care about me," Malila said. "If she did, she would send for me."

Malila's grandmother sighed and looked out at the river. "Sometimes the river is silent," she murmured. "It does not tell me what to say."

Chapter Four–

IT SEEMED TO MALILA as if she had lived in her grandmother's hut forever. She found it hard to remember her
life before, when she had played with other children in
the *soi*, the lane between the houses. The smell of jasmine, however, still made her think of her mother, and
sometimes in the market a man's quick smile brought
her father's face into her mind. But these things happened rarely.

Malila's new life was busy. She passed the days in her grandmother's company. Every morning she and Grandmother swept away the leaves in front of the hut and slapped the brooms against the plants looking for banded krait snakes, poisonous snakes whose bite could kill. If they found more than one snake, Grandmother sent word to the snake farmers. Men would come and light a small bonfire that attracted the snakes. They paid Malila's grandmother for the snakes they captured. The poisonous ones brought the most money.

Malila and her grandmother stayed to themselves. Grandmother did not speak to other shoppers in the market or people in the street. But they enjoyed their days together. They bought food and cooked. They shredded coconut to extract the milk. They picked water plants from the banks of the *klong* to make salads. They sang and told stories and prayed and observed the holy days. They went to the temple and purchased a carp or an ibis at the market near the temple, then released it as an act of goodness and to gain favor from the spirits.

More letters from America came, but Malila didn't ask about them. If her mother wasn't interested in sending for her, then Malila wasn't interested in hearing about her mother's struggles.

One day she came to her grandmother with a question.

"Grandmother, when we go to market, I see other children. I see them here too when I watch from the window."

"Yes, Malila."

"I see them playing together."

"Yes, Malila."

"Why don't I play with other children?"

Malila's grandmother put down her sewing.

"There are no children near our hut. You are too small to go far from the hut alone. Now, draw me a picture of a court dancer wearing a dress like the one I am making. It is for the *lakon nai*. It is a graceful dance, almost like a poem, and the dress must flow like a soft breeze."

Malila was not satisfied, but she could see that her grandmother did not wish to talk about this anymore. She nodded and began drawing.

One morning some weeks later, Malila heard an unfamiliar sound. Children were laughing! She ran to the window of the hut. Two little girls and four boys were playing at the edge of the canal. They splashed one another with water, then chased one another in a game of tag, squealing and giggling. They jumped into the water, tucking their legs and holding their noses, and swam and splashed like fish.

Malila was wide-eyed. Children! Playing just outside the porch! She slipped out of the door and watched the laughing children from the steps.

One girl saw Malila standing there. She turned to the others, whispering. All the children then stopped what they were doing and turned to look at Malila. She raised one hand and waved. They looked at one another, then turned their backs and resumed their play.

Malila stepped off the porch, easing closer to the children. They stopped giggling and splashing again. Malila smiled.

The oldest boy spoke to the others. Malila was too far away to understand his words, but after he spoke they all jumped into the water and swam away. Malila saw them get out of the water farther down the canal.

She watched them, wondering what she had done. She waved at them again when she saw them pointing at her. She heard their laughter.

"Malila, here you are. Why are you out here?" Malila's grandmother asked.

"Grandmother, those children ran away from me when I came outside. Why won't they play with me?"

"Their mothers confuse old ghosts with young children." Malila heard something in Grandmother's voice she had never heard before. Grandmother sounded almost angry.

Malila did not understand this but said nothing. She remembered that pain should be held tightly so it would not grow.

⁓

Malila made no attempt to approach other children again, and her grandmother did not encourage her. She watched them from the window as they passed. "Grandmother, why do these girls all wear the same clothes?" Malila asked one day.

Her grandmother came to the window and watched the girls going by. "Those are called uniforms, Malila. Those girls go to a special school that is very expensive."

"Will I go to such a school, Grandmother? Will I wear the uniform?" Malila felt a small glimmer of hope.

Malila's grandmother shook her head slowly. "Such a school would cost too much money. We would have to save for a long time even to travel to Bangkok to buy the uniform."

Malila smiled sadly as the hope faded. "*Mai pen rai*," she said. "Never mind."

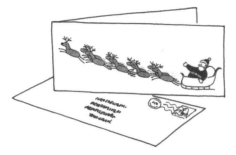

Not long after, the mailman brought another envelope. The outside was decorated with red flowers, and along the sides red and green letters spelled out SEASON'S GREETINGS. Neither Malila nor her grandmother knew the meaning of these words. The address was in Malila's mother's handwriting.

"This one is different," Malila said.

"Yes." Her grandmother opened the envelope very carefully and eased the card out. It showed a man in a red suit. He had a white beard and wore a cap. He was in a strange cart pulled by odd-looking deer. One deer had a shiny red nose.

Malila's grandmother opened the card. She began reading. "She says that America is beautiful and that her English is improving quickly. She has learned to drive an automobile! She says it is scary at first but exciting."

Malila's grandmother closed the card. "She hopes that you and I are very happy." She looked at Malila.

"Did she say when she would send for me?" The question was a low whisper. Malila was afraid she knew the answer, but she had to ask anyway.

"No, Malila."

Malila held back tears as she always did. She tossed her head. "Well, maybe we can write her and ask if she could send money for a uniform. Since she is driving an automobile, she must have money."

Her grandmother looked at the card in her hands for a long time. Finally, she said, "Sometimes we should wait and let hurt find us rather than invite it in." She put the card into the envelope.

Malila held the pain tight. "I understand," she said.

Malila spoke no more of school.

Three months later, on her seventh birthday, Malila woke to see a large package wrapped in brown paper next to her sleeping mat. On it were many strange stamps and something printed in the middle of the paper. She grabbed the box and went to find her grandmother.

"Grandmother, what is this? These stamps are like the ones on my mother's letters."

"Yes, Malila." Grandmother pointed to the writing on the paper. "This is your name. It means that the package is for you. It must be a present for your birthday."

Malila placed the box carefully on the floor. She pulled the wrapping away, folding it so that she could keep it. She took the top off the box and shuffled through wads of crumpled newspaper.

There were two presents. One was a framed picture. It showed a woman with long black hair. She stood in front of a blue automobile. She was smiling.

Malila looked up at her grandmother. "Is this . . . ?"

She let her voice trail off, then looked at the picture again.

"Yes, Malila. That is your mother. She looks very much like you, doesn't she?"

"I don't remember her this way. She seems smaller. She is pretty." Malila smiled at the picture, happy that her mother had remembered her.

She took out another small box. She held it up to show her grandmother.

"What is this?"

"That is called a camera. Your mother wrote to me about it. She says we are to take your picture with it. We can send the film to her and she will turn it into a picture of you."

"Has she forgotten what I look like?" Malila asked.

"I don't think so, but just as you thought she seems smaller, she will think you seem bigger."

Malila made a face. "I guess if she has a picture, she won't need me to come to America at all."

"Your mother sent you another present. But you must have my present before I give you hers." Grandmother went to the bamboo chest and brought out a box.

Malila held her breath, hoping she knew what was in the box but not daring to believe it. She had heard her grandmother sewing at night when Malila was supposed to be asleep. She had seen little scraps of dark material under the table. Malila was afraid that if she hoped too much, the box would somehow disappear the way her mother and father had.

She looked up at Grandmother. Grandmother smiled and with a small wave of her hand indicated that Malila should open the gift. Malila lifted the corner of the box and peeked in.

Malila moved the soft rice paper aside. Underneath was a school uniform. She flung back the paper and pulled out the white blouse and dark skirt.

"Oh, Grandmother! Thank you. It's beautiful."

"Your mother sent money to pay for tuition. Now you will go to school. You will make your ancestors smile with pride." Malila's grandmother opened her arms. She gathered Malila into a long hug.

Chapter Five~

MALILA DRESSED IN HER NEW UNIFORM on her first day of school. Her grandmother took her photograph with the camera that her mother had sent.

"Let me take your picture too," Malila said. "Stand next to the spirit house and be sure to smile." Malila took the picture, then handed the camera to her grandmother.

"I will send this film to your mother. She will be very proud to see you in your uniform."

Malila was excited to go to school at last. She was also frightened to leave her grandmother and the safe, quiet house.

Malila's grandmother walked with her to school. They walked along the canals, watching the vendors paddle their way to the marketplace. They passed the market where the barefoot shopkeepers were setting out their wares. Gaily colored parasols shaded the open-air booths.

Malila's school was in a *wat*. Her grandmother stopped outside the door and faced Malila.

"You are the daughter of your ancestors. Your blood is thick with the lives of those before you. Carry your name with pride." She folded her hands in front of her and made the *wai*. She turned and walked away.

Grandmother had never made this gesture to Malila before. It was a sign of respect. Filled with pride, Malila straightened her shoulders and walked into the yard.

The other children were laughing and playing. They all seemed to know one another. A tall man with black hair and mahogany skin, wearing the long dark robe of a teacher, came into the yard and rang a bell. All the children began filing into the schoolroom. Malila took a desk in the back of the room. The teacher called roll.

"Suwanna Ngy."

A small girl in the front of the room stood up. The

teacher smiled and nodded. The girl sat down again.

"Thi Dao."

"Lan Nyk."

"Namtian Chu."

"Tiana Walonyisan."

"Pai Lom."

Each of the girls rose, received her smile and acknowledgment, and sat down.

"Malila Noi Phai."

Malila stood, nervous but smiling.

"Are you the daughter of Sulaksana?" he asked. Malila nodded yes, excited that someone knew her father.

The teacher's face grew very stern. He looked at Malila as if he had a bad taste in his mouth. "Sit down, please."

Two children began whispering. They turned and stared at her.

"Look at her uniform," said one girl. "It's homemade."

Another girl snickered. "Don't you know who she is?" She bent over and whispered. The first girl's eyes became round and she stared at Malila rudely.

Malila was bewildered. Why did the teacher and those children look at her that way?

The teacher rapped on his desk with a wooden stick. "Quiet, girls. Get out your paper and your pencils. We will learn to make the characters you will use for writing.

Please copy them neatly and carefully." He began writing characters on the board.

Malila began copying the characters. She noticed the other children sneaking looks at her once again. She could not concentrate. She wondered what was wrong with her that they stared at her so. She felt embarrassed. As the teacher talked about vowels and tonal sounds, she began to draw a lovely princess on her paper. The princess had many friends around her, looking at her in admiration.

Suddenly, Malila's paper was snatched from in front of her. Her teacher was glaring at her drawing.

"This is not how you learn to write! Pay attention!"

The teacher tore Malila's paper into pieces. The other children whispered and giggled. Malila hung her head. Her cheeks flamed and her eyes stung with tears. She pulled out another piece of paper and began copying the characters again. Slowly. Miserably.

At noon, the children were let out into the yard to play. A group of girls were sitting on the ground playing *ee tak*. They took turns using a paper scoop to pick up one fruit seed at a time from a pile without moving the others. Malila saw one of the girls whisper to another.

"May I play?" Malila asked.

The girl who had whispered shook her head. "My mother told me not to play with you."

Malila did not understand, but she left and walked over to a circle of girls who were kicking a ball made of strips of rattan. The game was called *takraw,* and Malila remembered having such a ball before her father died.

Suddenly one of the girls pointed at Malila and called her a name. Another girl threw a wad of gum at Malila. It landed in her long, straight hair, making a knot right in front that she could not get out.

Malila was stunned. To touch the head of another was taboo. The personal spirit resided in the head. It was the worst possible insult.

"Why did you do that?" she cried. "I have done nothing to you."

"You don't belong here," one girl shouted.

"You can't even afford a proper uniform. Your grandmother is a poor seamstress," another girl sneered.

"Gangster girl!" one called. "Thief's baby!"

"What do you mean?" Malila asked. "Why do you call me these names?"

"Your father was in the gangs," the girl who threw the gum shouted at her. "He was a thief. The police shot him in the streets like a dog!"

"No," Malila said, "my father was a good man. He . . . he . . ." Malila faltered. She did not know anything about her father. Her grandmother always said that he was a good man and that he had just died suddenly. But she remembered the policeman talking to her mother. She remembered the neighbors staring and whispering when they walked to her grandmother's house. She remembered that despite what her mother had said about making arrangements, there was never a funeral. She remembered how her mother had left so quickly without even saying good-bye.

Malila's stomach gathered into a cold knot as she realized that what these girls said might be true. When she saw the hate in their eyes, she knew that it must be true. Her stomach hurt and her head swam.

"None of us want you here." Only one girl said the words, but Malila knew that all the others agreed.

The teacher appeared. He rang the bell and summoned the children back to class. Malila stood in the dusty play yard after the others had gone inside.

"Are you going in?" the stern man asked.

"They don't want me to play with them." Malila's voice was small. It wasn't what she wanted to say, but she couldn't ask the disapproving man the questions that pounded in her head.

"You seem surprised," the teacher said. "This is a small village and many people remember your father. I remember him. Why are you surprised that the other children don't want you around? The village elder pronounced your family *suay*."

Malila stared at him. "*Suay?*" She looked away, confused. "Unlucky?" She looked back at the teacher. "I don't understand. How can the elder tell me that I'm unlucky?"

The teacher's voice was cold. "Has your grandmother told you nothing? When the elder pronounces a family *suay,* they are to be shunned. Your father was a criminal. He died a criminal's death. No one wants any part of your father's bad luck."

It was as if Malila's father had been taken from her twice. She was left with nothing.

She would not cry in front of this scornful teacher. "*Mai pen rai,*" she said. "Never mind. Never mind." She lifted her chin, turned, and walked away from the school.

Chapter Six~

MALILA DID NOT GO STRAIGHT HOME. She walked through the village to the forest beyond, to be alone with her thoughts of her father.

As she wandered among the trees, huge elephants that worked in the teak forests lumbered past. Malila sat beside a teak tree and bowed her head.

"Father, I loved you," she said aloud, her voice rough with tears. "Now I learn you are a bad man and a thief. People hate me because of you. What am I supposed to do? Why did you leave me alone like this?" Malila's tears fell on the dark skirt of her school uniform. Elephants trumpeted deep in the forest.

Evening came and the sky darkened. Malila heard soft footsteps. She looked up to see her grandmother.

"Malila, I believe the dragon has breathed upon you today," Grandmother said. She leaned down and took Malila's hands, pulled Malila to her feet, and hugged her. "The dragon's breath brings great pain and sorrow, but it can turn coal into diamond. Come home with me now."

Malila nodded her head. Her tears ran down her face. She looked back at her father's grave.

"Was my father a thief?"

Her grandmother nodded slowly.

"Was he shot in the streets by the police?"

"Yes."

"Do you still love him after what he did?"

"Yes. I have blamed myself for his failings. I thought I did all of the correct things. When I was waiting for his birth, I walked under the belly of an elephant, as the old ones tell us to do for good luck in the birth. I dressed him in cloth with the drawing of the giant Taowetsuwan to protect him from evil spirits. His father and I performed the rituals of respect by dipping a coconut in oil, then the baby in water. We put a cat in his crib. He wore the traditional head knot of hair to ward off illness."

She sighed and shook her head as if weary. "But I believe that at his birth the Chao Thi was angry and sent demons to lead him astray. He paid for his sins with his life. I cannot hate him. I believe my love will help him be a better man in his next life."

"But I am a gangster's child. How can you love me?"

"To love you is not a *tam boon*; it's not a sacrifice. It is a joy and an honor."

Malila and her grandmother walked home under the stars.

—

Grandmother cut Malila's hair in bangs to remove the gum. When Malila looked in the mirror, her large, dark eyes glowed beneath the silky bangs.

Malila's grandmother said, "We have performed the special ritual that will call the head *khwan* that was insulted back into your body. The bangs make you more beautiful. When you return to school, the children will see that a spirit protects you. They will know that their cruelty cannot harm you."

"Grandmother, I don't want to go back there. The children made fun of my clothes and they called me names."

Malila's grandmother was quiet for a long time.

"Malila," she whispered at last, "I should have warned you that this might happen. But the world is changing, and I thought old superstitions might be forgotten. I was wrong. The village is small and it changes very little. It is not your fault, but for you a life in this village will be rooted in misery. You must find the skills to help you leave it. You can only find those in school."

"But Grandmother, the teacher thinks I am stupid."

"And you shall learn to read and write and prove him wrong. One who knows how to live may walk among the tigers."

―

Malila went back to school the next day. She took her place in the back of the room. She ignored the whispers and giggles. She stood politely when her name was called for roll and answered in a quiet, respectful voice.

Malila was copying her letters carefully and slowly when suddenly a ruler flashed across her desk and rapped her knuckles.

"This paper is messy and careless!" The teacher rapped her knuckles again. "Do it over. You cannot be lazy in my class!"

Malila caught her trembling lip between her teeth and rubbed her knuckles. She began her work again, concentrating harder, making the letters perfect.

Later, the teacher called on Malila with a question. She did not know the answer. Looking around her, confused and embarrassed, she saw only unfriendly faces. Her own face flushed, but she held her head high when she stood.

"I'm sorry. I don't know the answer."

The silence hung in the air as if the whole class were holding its breath.

"Well, class, Malila does not know the answer. Why do you think she does not know the answer?" He looked around the room with a cruel smile on his face. The students looked at one another, then stared at Malila. She felt like a slow and ugly beetle being watched by a hungry cat.

"I will tell you why Malila does not know the answer. She is a daydreamer! Daydreamers do not learn, Malila."

"No, sir," Malila said clearly. "I shall try harder, sir."

"See that you do. Take your seat."

—

Malila went back to school the next day and the next and the days that followed. She was shunned by the others. She felt the dragon's breath again and again.

When they had art class the teacher picked up her drawing.

"Malila, this is no good. It is plain that you have no

talent. You should concentrate on learning a good trade like weaving baskets or carving fruit." He flung the paper down in disgust.

Malila picked up the drawing and continued to work on it. "*Mai pen rai,*" she whispered to herself. "Never mind. Never mind."

Chapter Seven~

ONE SPRING EVENING, Malila sat on her stool on the porch. The stars were just beginning to appear and the breezes were soft against her cheek. Malila watched the river and listened to its music. Storks and egrets waded along the banks, their necks curved in graceful arcs as they hunted small fish. The heat was gone from the day, chased away by the evening breeze. It was a tranquil time of day, called buffalo afternoon because the water buffalo were unhitched from their burdens and permitted to roll and wallow in the mud. Then the farmers would lead their buffalo home, usually with children riding the beasts' broad backs.

Grandmother came out of the hut carrying something in her hand.

"Malila, this came today while you were in school." She held out a white square.

Malila sighed. "A letter from my mother," she said.

"Yes." Her grandmother looked sad and worried.

Malila patted her grandmother's hand. "Don't be upset, Grandmother. I know that it's not a letter asking me to come to America."

"No, Malila. She does not ask for you."

"Good," Malila said. "I don't want to go. I like my life here with you." Her throat felt tight.

"She has other news, Malila."

Malila looked at the evening sky, trying to bring back her earlier sense of peace. "Has she gotten a new automobile?"

"No. She has gotten a new husband." Malila's grandmother sat down on her stool. Malila kept looking at the stars. She did not turn her head.

Her grandmother continued. "She writes that she married some time ago. She says she is very happy."

Malila said nothing.

"Your mother is young, Malila. Her time in Thailand was full of pain and hurt. She wants to forget that hurt."

"So she forgets me as well."

"She is not yet at peace with her life, Malila. She does not walk with the tigers. Maybe someday you will show her how."

Malila grabbed the letter and tore it into little pieces. She flung them into the river. "My mother will have to learn from her new husband," Malila said. "She is a *farang*, a Westerner, now. And I live in Thailand."

"And maybe that is your joy and her sorrow."

Grandmother took Malila's hand and turned the palm up to the stars. She traced her finger lightly along a crease.

"This is your life line, Malila. See how it is broken with many branches?"

Malila looked. "What does that mean? Will my life be full of broken things?"

Her grandmother smiled. "In a way, yes. But it also means that your life will have many new beginnings. The river says that things do not happen as we expect them to."

This time Malila laughed and she took her grandmother's hand and kissed it. "The river has said that before, Grandmother."

"And the river never lies."

Malila listened to the river often in the days and months that followed. She read her mother's letters without much comment. She went to school, lived her life, and hoped for little. The less she hoped for, the less she would be disappointed. Her life was calm, and if not happy, she was content.

Malila worked hard at school to make her grandmother proud, but she found little satisfaction in her good grades. The year she was ten, each student was assigned to pick a festival and write a paper explaining its history and the meaning of its activities.

Malila chose the king's birthday and the *fawn lep* dance as one of its highlights. She wrote that the *fawn lep* must be danced by young unmarried girls. They wear curved brass tips on their fingernails. As cymbals and gongs play a slow song, the dancers wave the fingernails about their faces to represent water orchids floating on the water. Malila wrote about the young men who dance around the silk-draped girls but are not allowed to touch them. She wrote that the orchid is a symbol of purity and innocence. Innocence, like the orchid, is fragile. Touching an orchid causes it to bruise and blacken, hastening its death. The dance reminds people that purity of thought and action is necessary for a good life.

The day the teacher returned the paper, Malila got a surprise. The stern-faced man told the class, "I will read the best one. It is excellent. The facts are accurate and the writing is well organized." He began reading Malila's paper.

Malila's face flamed and her eyes smarted with tears. She had never been praised in school before.

When the teacher finished reading the paper, some of the girls began clapping. The teacher cleared his throat, a signal for quiet. "The paper is Malila's." There was no more clapping. A few girls grumbled. No one looked at Malila as the teacher glided over and dropped the paper on her desk. "The paper is good. I suppose your grandmother helped you with it."

Malila was crushed. Because her father had been a criminal, she always would always be suspected of wrongdoing. She took the paper home and threw it away.

That evening, Grandmother came into her sleeping room carrying the discarded paper.

"Malila, I found this in the box with my scraps. This is a lovely paper, and you were given high marks. Why didn't you show it to me?"

Malila told her what the teacher had said and how the other girls had smirked and whispered.

Grandmother sighed. Malila could see that she had no wisdom to offer her. They sat in silence.

Malila thought, I shouldn't even try. Making good grades makes no difference. No matter what I do, I'm still *suay*.

———

One day in late March, Grandmother returned from market carrying a flyer. "Malila, we're going to have an adventure," she said. "There is a kite-flying contest in the next village on Saturday. We shall go there."

At this time of year, both children and adults flew kites. In the afternoon a steady southwest monsoon scattered the heat and sent bamboo and rice paper fantasies to dance with the clouds. The kites were homemade and no two were alike. They were made to resemble birds, fish, or butterflies. Malila had made and flown her own kite often enough.

"Why is it so important that I see kites in another village? You're being mysterious." Malila wrinkled her nose. "Am I about to get some more Buddhist wisdom?"

"Hush, child. You've gotten a sharp tongue along with your long legs." Grandmother smiled and carried her market basket into the kitchen. "I want to enjoy the good weather. We need to get out of this house and this village for a day."

Malila followed. "You mean you want to have fun, just like other people?"

"Yes, have fun. Just like other people. You are too serious. Does the idea of having fun scare you?" She put the basket on the table, then placed her hands on her hips, as though challenging Malila.

"No, I'm not scared to have fun," Malila said. But she was not quite sure it was true.

"Good," Grandmother said. "It's settled."

On Saturday, Malila and her grandmother got on the small bus that shuttled between villages. Malila had never been farther than the *wat* and the market, and she found the unfamiliar sights a little frightening but fascinating. From the windows of the chugging bus she watched the farmers' ox-drawn carts and the cars. Occasionally an army jeep or transport truck full of khaki-clad soldiers sped by, churning up dust.

"Grandmother, where are those soldiers going?"

Grandmother sighed. "We must hope they are just on training maneuvers."

"My grandfather was in the army, wasn't he?"

Grandmother's expression turned wistful. "Yes, he was so handsome in his uniform. We lived near the base, closer to Bangkok. That is where my sewing was noticed by the court. I made some costumes for the officers' wives. . . ." Her voice drifted away and she watched the road pass by through the window of the bus. After a moment, Malila touched her grandmother's knee.

Grandmother looked away from the window and into Malila's face. "I was thinking of other times. Times when I thought I would always be young and lovely." She smiled and waved her hand as if sending thoughts of herself out of the bus window.

"Anyway, there was a coup in one of the southern provinces. It seems there is a coup every four or five years, but it always ends the same. The military comes in, the coup is over, and our king is still our ruler. Only in this coup, some soldiers were killed. Your grandfather was one of them. He died when your father was younger than you are now.

"I moved back to the village where I had grown up. The hut we live in was my mother's. I always missed the river when I lived in the city."

Grandmother looked sad. Malila decided to change the subject. "Tell me about this kite contest."

"I think I can show you. Look, we're here."

They got off the hot, crowded bus and began walking through the village. "The contest grounds are not far. And the breeze is picking up now. We will be just in time," Grandmother said.

At the contest grounds, crowds of people were chattering and several small bands were playing. Malila thought she had never seen so many people or heard so much noise in one place. There were kites everywhere:

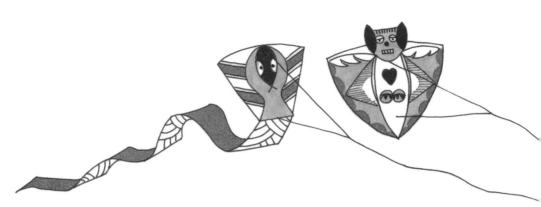

kites made like centipedes, serpents, and peacocks. Vividly colored butterflies swooped past kite frogs that leaped in the air over fluttering carp. The sky was a riot of fish and fowl, bright spots of scarlet, yellow, green, and purple against the brilliant blue sky and billowing white clouds. Malila felt hollow inside at the sight of so much beauty.

"I must remember all of this and draw it when we go home," she said.

"There is more. Let us find a good place. The teams are coming onto the field."

A few men cleared a space in the middle of the grounds. "Those are the umpires. They will watch the teams and the kites to see if they are abiding by the rules," Grandmother said.

Next, a group of fifteen men came onto the field. They carried a huge kite. They were followed by a team of only three men who carried a small kite.

"The great star-shaped kite is the *chula,* the male kite," Grandmother explained. "Some call it the dragon kite because it is so large and fierce. The tiny kite is the *pakpao,* the female kite. It is shaped like a diamond because while it is small, it is hard and enduring, like a diamond."

They watched as the teams studied the skies, then released their kites to the gusts.

"The big kite flies into the small kite's territory and tries to grab it with its bamboo talons. They fight until one kite or the other crashes to the ground. It is a battle to the death."

The bands came to the edge of the field. Each band picked the kite it would support and played for its victory. The drums thudded, the cymbals clashed, and the Java pipes screamed as the huge dragon kite rose on the steady monsoon wind and pulled against its strings. It raced the clouds, charging through the air, straining to reach the tiny kite.

Malila thought the dragon kite looked huge and fierce. The battle seemed so unfair.

The *pakpao* darted about in its home territory, dodging the powerful male kite. The *chula* climbed and reared and plunged. The small kite dipped and dodged, but it appeared to be losing the battle.

Malila's throat was tight and she clenched her hands. She knew that the large kite would bring the small kite crashing to the ground. Why had grandmother brought her here?

The *chula* reared on the breeze, its curved bamboo talons ready, when, suddenly, the *pakpao* stopped running. It trembled in the sky, then swooped down and around. It streaked up and flashed in the sunshine. The small kite had wrapped its line around the huge star. The *chula* lost its strength and tumbled to the ground.

Malila cheered for the little kite. Grandmother cheered too.

"Did you bring me here to teach me a lesson?" Malila asked Grandmother as the applause continued around them. "How could you know the little kite would win?"

Grandmother smiled. "I didn't. I wanted us to have a good time." Grandmother had stopped clapping, but her smile was bigger than ever. "But it would be silly to ignore a sign. The little kite's winning today seems lucky, don't you think?"

"Yes. We were lucky today." Malila smiled and looked at the sky. The sun was warm on her face.

Chapter Eight

MALILA WASN'T SURE WHAT HAD CHANGED, but she found she was happier. She picked flowers until the small hut was filled with the heady smells of canna, hibiscus, and magnolia gathered into makeshift vases, and brightened the walls with her pictures of flowers, water buffalo, and market boats.

Malila discovered a new side of Grandmother. She wasn't always wise and serious; she sometimes said things that made Malila laugh.

One day as Malila was drawing a picture of her grandmother pulling a fish from a trap, she said, "Grandmother, Buddha tells us that we should not take any creature's life. How can we kill this fish?"

Grandmother said, "This fish was stupid to enter this trap and die. I didn't kill it. I just took this stupid fish from the water. If an animal dies, does it matter who eats it?"

Malila changed Grandmother's serious expression in the picture and drew in an impish grin.

Malila had always loved the rainy season that followed the hot months of February to May. This year it seemed especially refreshing. Late in May, thunderstorms brought huge raindrops that fell on the hard earth with loud plops. The ground hissed and steamed as it soaked in the tropical rain. Then the monsoons came. The rain fell in thick sheets, causing the rivers to overflow. As the lanes and streets became rivers themselves, Malila had the feeling that she was safe on an island, isolated by the walls of water.

During the rainy season there was no school, and Malila helped her grandmother with the sewing. The many festivals kept Grandmother busy. A messenger from the court would arrive with packages of silks, threads, beads, and sketches of costumes. Grandmother would look at the drawings, cut patterns, and begin to sew. Weeks later another messenger would arrive to collect the dresses and bring new fabrics.

Malila packed finished costumes, folding the delicate fabrics between layers of rice paper. "Grandmother, don't you wish you were royalty and could wear these beautiful things?" she asked one day.

Grandmother's answer came quickly. "No, never."

"Why not?"

"I would rather be the person who creates beauty than the one who simply wears it."

Malila smiled. "You always have the answer. What would I ever do without you?"

Grandmother's serene expression turned serious. "Someday you may have to. Then you'll find your own answers."

The costumes for Tod Kathin were complete by the end of the rainy season, and Grandmother had a break from her work for the court. Malila was puzzled when Grandmother bought yards of saffron-colored cotton and began cutting them into lengths and hemming them. She worked quietly, and Malila thought she looked troubled.

"Grandmother, what are you making now?" Malila asked. "Those look like the robes the monks wear."

"Malila, I have been a poor grandmother. I have kept you too much to myself. It was selfish. And I may not always be with you. I think it is time for us to join in the festivities of this village."

"Grandmother, have you forgotten the lessons you taught me?" Malila crossed her arms over her chest. "You told me that sometimes we should wait and let hurt find us rather than invite it in."

Grandmother narrowed her eyes at Malila. "I said 'sometimes.' This is not one of those times. And I might have been wrong. It could happen, you know." She folded the cloth almost fiercely.

"But we are *suay*," Malila said. "Why go to a festival to be shunned again?"

Grandmother stopped folding the cloth and shook her head. "Just because the village elder proclaims us unlucky, it doesn't make it true." She paused and turned to face Malila. "I'm not certain that we will be shunned. I've never given anyone the chance to treat us different-ly. I may have been the one who has done the shunning. It's time to find out." She turned back to her work. "Tomorrow is Tod Kathin, and we will take these new robes to the monks."

"Maybe this is one of the times you are wrong," Malila said. "It could happen, you know."

"Sometimes you learn too well." Grandmother folded the last robe and motioned for Malila to sit down. "Stop arguing with your old grandmother. I will tell you about the festival in Bangkok. It is much bigger and very beautiful there."

Malila sat. She knew that her grandmother's mind was made up. They would go to the festival.

"It starts the same in Bangkok as it does here. The people take robes to the monks. Then great crowds go to the river to watch the Royal Barge Procession. Boats that are one hundred feet long with prows carved like the sacred swan and the great serpents glide along the river. Each boat is rowed by sixty men all robed in scarlet."

"I don't remember you making scarlet robes for the court."

"No, those robes don't have any decoration. I made the ornate robe that the king wears." Grandmother paused. "Where was I?"

"The boats and the rowers all in scarlet robes. Where do the boats go, Grandmother?"

"They carry the king on a golden throne to the Grand Palace. There he brings offerings to the monks at the Temple of the Emerald Buddha.

"What is the Emerald Buddha?"

"It is the most sacred Buddha, a gift from the gods. No one knows for certain where the Buddha comes from. It is decorated with jade. Because of the green, the people called it the Emerald Buddha. It sits high on a golden altar and it seems to glow. The king changes the Buddha's robes three times a year. It wears a diamond-studded tunic in the hot season and a gilded blue robe for the rainy season, and during Tod Kathin, a solid gold robe for the cold season."

"Oh Grandmother, how beautiful it must be!" Malila said. "Why go to a silly little festival here when the one in Bangkok must be so beautiful?"

"Yes, it is quite beautiful, Malila. But the beauty of the ceremony is not as important as the true meaning of the holy day. All the festivals involve the spirit of giving. We have always observed the holy days alone in our hut. This year we will join the village and take cowrie shells, *arica* nuts, and flowers to the local *wat*. When you give, you are equal with the king."

The next morning, Malila and Grandmother took the robes and other offerings to the *wat*. No one spoke directly to them, but none of the villagers were rude.

"Grandmother, why do the girls at school treat me so badly, even though no one here is impolite?" Malila asked on the way home.

"People have busy lives of their own. Maybe they have forgotten about your father. The girls at school see you every day, and they treat you badly out of habit."

Malila and her grandmother began to go into the village more often. Grandmother would nod to some of the neighbors. At first this small greeting was met with looks of surprise, but in time one person and then another nodded in return.

On the night before the New Year, Grandmother came into Malila's sleeping room and sat next to her. "Malila, tomorrow is the festival of Songkran. Do you know about this festival?"

"We studied it in school. The teacher said that it is called 'the bathing of the Buddha.' He said that to show acceptance of man's lowly status, the faithful must wash the feet of Buddha. Since we can't wash the real Buddha, the young wash the feet of their elders, and everyone goes to the *wat* to wash the feet of the monks."

"Yes, and then there is a wonderful festival in the streets. I think we will be accepted if we go. At least we must try."

In the morning, Malila awakened her grandmother and, with formality, "bathed" her, gently washing her feet with a large sponge.

"Grandmother, don't laugh. This part of Songkran is very serious."

"Yes, but you're tickling my feet. The gods are laughing too, Malila. Don't you hear them?" The teak temple bells were tinkling gaily in the morning air, calling the worshipers to the *wat*.

Malila and her grandmother joined the crowds in the

street. All the people wore the many-hued traditional clothes and carried rice, fruits, candies, and flowers as gifts for the monks. Each person, young and old, sprinkled water on the Buddha and the abbot as a ceremonial bath. Malila saw that very few people avoided them and some even smiled and nodded.

Outside the *wat*, a parade snaked through the streets. Many musicians played Java pipes, cymbals, gongs, and large drums. The village maidens of marriageable age wore bright pink blouses covered with tiny orchids. They splashed water from silver bowls onto the people in the crowd and the parade. The maidens were encouraged to flirt and play but never to touch another person, especially a male. It was a Thai taboo.

Malila and her grandmother joined the fun. "Look, Grandmother!" Malila exclaimed, pointing to several young men who danced the *ramwong,* a folk dance. Tied onto their fingertips were tiny cymbals, and the men thumped these together at each step. They were followed by a team of slender girls in wine-red costumes dancing the dreamy *fawn lep*. They waved long brass-tipped fingernails in time to the slow pounding of cymbals and gongs.

Malila shrieked as a skinny man dressed as a policeman dashed water down her neck. He danced a jig around the float of the Songkran maidens while giggling

women squirted water in the faces of the males in the crowd. Merry-makers all around them splashed water on one another in a sprightly imitation of the bathing ceremony. Grown-ups and children stood in the river, hurling water at everyone in sight.

A monk approached and greeted them. *"Sawatdee pimai."*

"Happy New Year," Malila and Grandmother said, and reverently sprinkled a few drops of water on the monk's robe.

Malila and her grandmother returned home soaking wet and laughing.

"Malila, look at me. I am too old for this foolishness!" her grandmother said. Malila knew Grandmother was thrilled that people had thrown water on them.

"Mai pen rai," Malila said, giggling. "Never mind. Never mind."

Chapter Nine~

THE NEXT YEAR, Malila went to school at a different *wat*. She had progressed to a school for older girls in the neighboring village. She had new classmates, from other nearby villages, and new teachers. Some of the new girls did not know about Malila's father and were friendly at first, but Malila did not know how to talk to these girls. She knew only one way to behave—silent and apart from others. Soon they stopped trying to include her.

One of the teachers talked in a smooth, musical voice and was kind and patient with everyone, even Malila. He was especially encouraging during art classes. He would look at each girl's work and say something pleasant. "That is very good," he told one girl with a nod and a smile. "Your brush strokes are improving. Keep it up," he said to another.

When he stopped and watched Malila draw or paint, he always stood quiet for a long while. Then he would smile at Malila and move on to another girl without saying anything. Malila tried hard to paint as the other girls did, laboring over her pictures of teacups, glass bottles, small dogs, or fluffy cats, but the teacher only smiled and remained silent.

Malila sighed when this happened. *Soon he'll tell me to concentrate on carving fruit and making baskets too,* she thought each time. *He'll just say it nicer.*

One day, the teacher reached out and took her brush. "Malila, you draw very nicely, but nothing seems to have life," he said.

Malila lowered her head, miserable. This was the rejection she had been expecting. "The other teacher also told me I had no talent," she said.

"The other teacher must be mistaken. You certainly have talent. But you just copy what the other girls do. Your paintings have no spirit." He took away the paper she was writing on and gave her a fresh new sheet.

Malila was confused and surprised. She could not take in what he said. Talent. Had he said she had talent?

"Do you draw or paint at home?"

"Yes."

"What do you draw?"

Malila lowered her head further. "The pictures are unworthy. My grandmother tells me stories, and I draw what I think the story would look like."

Malila kept her eyes down, but when the teacher made no response she stole a glance at his face. To her surprise, he was smiling. "I like stories," he said. "What kind of stories does she tell?"

Malila tried to smile in return. "Oh, when she sews, she tells me about the ceremonies and I draw the dancers in their costumes."

"Ah," the teacher said, handing the brush back to Malila. "Then we shall experiment. I shall tell you a story and you will paint."

Malila took the brush and stared at the blank paper.

"Have you ever been to a kick-boxing match?"

"No," Malila said. "But I have heard of them, and I've seen posters in the village."

"Good. Now, let me explain. Thai kick boxing is a wonderful event. The ring is square and bounded by ropes. There is an orchestra next to it. One man plays a xylophone made of bamboo. Set in a circle around the musicians are gongs. Each one makes a different sound. Another man plays a Java pipe. The idea is that the music speeds up the blood and brings the spirits to the fighters. The music gets faster and louder as the boxing match goes on."

Malila made a few hesitant gestures toward the paper with the brush, then laid the brush down. When she drew pictures of Grandmother's stories, she had always used chalk or charcoal. She grabbed a stick of charcoal and began sketching quickly, first the man with the Java pipe, then the other musicians and the gongs. Her charcoal flew and her eyes widened as she tried to keep up with the teacher's words.

"First, you see, the fighters dance around the ring to the music. They are showing the people and the spirits their style of boxing. Then each boxer gives thanks to his trainer. He gets on his knees and faces the direction of his birthplace and makes the *krap* to show respect. After that he does a dance. He stays on his knees and sways his head and arms. He can make gestures that will 'hex' his opponent."

Malila drew the boxer on his knees, bowing low.

The teacher pointed to the drawing. "There, on the boxer's arm, he ties on an amulet to bring him good luck

and keep him from serious injury. He wears boxing shorts and gloves, but he is barefoot so he can kick with his feet. On his head he wears a sacred headband."

Malila changed the slippered feet of her boxer to bare feet and sketched in the amulet and headband.

She was drawing too fast to feel self-conscious. This was very much like drawing while Grandmother told stories.

"Over here, in the ring, draw two fighters. Show one kicking. They can kick anywhere on the body, and the kick is very hard. Sometimes it can be heard across the stadium.

"Oh, it is such a spectacle! It looks like a murder is going on, but no Thai fighter will ever admit to being hurt. A good Thai boxer can jump several feet into the air, and he is allowed to slam his opponent on his chin or in the ribs or stomach. He whips his foot around in a wide arc and with the speed of a lightning bolt he will kick his opponent on the ear."

Caught up in his story, the teacher rubbed his hands together, then pointed to the picture again. "And now, the musicians play faster and louder and the fans begin screaming. If they want to see elbow ramming, they cry *'Sok! Sok!'* and if they want to see the knee blow, they shout *'Kow! Kow!'*"

Malila sketched in expressions on the boxers' faces

and then began filling in the spectators outside the ring, cheering and waving their arms around.

Suddenly she noticed that the teacher was no longer speaking. She turned around to see the entire class grouped behind him, staring silently at her picture.

The teacher reached over and pulled the picture from the easel. "Now, this has spirit. It has life. This is art."

Some of the girls murmured and grumbled and turned away but a few of them continued looking at the picture.

"This is really good, Malila," said one girl, smiling.

"Yes, you should do more things like this," said another.

"Thank you," Malila said. Other than Grandmother, no one had ever given Malila a compliment. "Thank you, too," she said to her teacher.

—

At the next art class, Malila picked up her pencils and stared at the empty paper until the teacher appeared behind her. "I don't think I can draw unless you tell me a story," Malila told him.

"I think you can, Malila. Don't worry about the other students. Draw the things that call to your heart."

Malila was bewildered, but she nodded to the teacher. When he had moved on, she took a deep breath. "Thi?" she said softly.

The girl at the next easel turned to her. "Yes, Malila."

"Can you help me? I don't understand what he means. Last time I drew a picture of a kick-boxing match. Does he want me to do that again? What do you think he means about things that call to my heart?"

Malila held her breath, waiting for Thi to laugh and say something unkind, but the girl merely furrowed her brow and scratched at the side of her face with the wooden end of her brush.

"I think that kick boxing was something that called to *his* heart," she said at last. "Something he loves and understands. Maybe he wants you to paint something you love and understand."

Malila was still puzzled.

Thi sighed. "I'm not saying this very well." She tapped the brush against her temple. "Try it this way. Think of a time when you were very happy or maybe very sad, and paint a picture that shows that feeling."

"So," Malila said, "when he sees the picture he wants to feel what's inside it, not just look at something pretty."

Thi flashed a bright smile. "That's it. That's exactly what I meant."

"Thank you," Malila said.

"Anytime," Thi said as she returned to her painting.

Malila began a pencil drawing. She worked on it for several days before turning it in. The drawing was of an old woman and a young girl placing a rope of jasmine and orchid blooms on the roof of a spirit house. A canal with market boats was in the background.

"Ah, Malila. You are truly a child of Thailand," the teacher said, holding up the drawing. "You have caught the soul of our country. You drew from your heart this time. You have been given a great gift. Do not lose sight of it again."

A child of Thailand, Malila thought. Yes, I am a child of Thailand. She glanced over and saw Thi smile at her.

Chapter Ten

WHEN MALILA WAS FOURTEEN, her grandmother became ill. At first she simply was very tired at the end of the day. Malila worried about her, but her grandmother dismissed it. "It is nothing, Malila. I am an old woman. I shall begin taking a little nap in the afternoon." Malila started doing the cooking and the cleaning to help her grandmother.

In a few weeks Malila noticed that her grandmother

could not keep up with the sewing. "My fingers are getting slow, Malila," Grandmother admitted. "I cannot make these tiny stitches as quickly as I used to. My naps seem to be getting longer."

"Do not worry, Grandmother. Go to bed now and rest. I will finish this costume for you."

Malila's grandmother looked at her with sad eyes. "Yes, you will finish for me. You will take over what I cannot do."

As the weeks went on, Malila's grandmother was able to do less and less, so Malila did more and more. Every week she stewed a chicken to make stock and mixed it with cooked rice, egg, ginger, and coriander leaves to make *kao dom,* a rice soup that was often given to children and invalids because it was so easily digestible. She urged her grandmother to eat and rest so that she could regain her strength.

Finally Malila stayed home from school to take care of her grandmother and do the sewing. Her grandmother's naps grew longer and longer. When the sewing was done, while her grandmother slept, Malila drew and painted.

She painted temple bells swinging in the wind, women in pink silk smiling and laughing, jungle tigers roaring, wooden sandals clacking against teak floors, and vendors crying out news of their wares. She painted the

slowness of the water buffalo, the arched necks of the egrets, and the elegance of the soaring prow of the Royal Barge. She painted the mystery of the jungle and the strength of the mountain peaks. She painted the loneliness of the sunset and the longing of the river. And she painted the people: princesses in blue silk dresses, monks in saffron robes, court ladies in ornate costumes, festival dancers in wine-red sarongs, and children riding on the broad backs of the buffalo.

Malila thought about her teacher's words. "You have been given a great gift." She had painted what was in her heart.

One evening, while Grandmother slept, Malila looked at her paintings, then went outside to listen to the river.

"River," she said quietly, "I was given a gift. Do you know what it was?"

The river rippled and gurgled and murmured. *Thailand,* it whispered. *Thailand.*

Malila nodded to the river. "Yes, I think so too. Who gave me this gift? Do you know that, river? Can you tell me?"

And the river told Malila.

Malila smiled sadly. "Yes, my mother gave me to my grandmother and my grandmother gave me Thailand. I know that the river never lies. You tell me the truth that

I have refused to see." She went inside and wrote a letter to her mother.

—

Soon, Malila's grandmother could no longer rise from her sleeping mat. Malila missed school, but she was determined to take care of Grandmother. Malila did all the housework and cared for her grandmother in every way. She did all the sewing for the costumes. When she sewed, she would sit by her grandmother's sleeping mat, and now she would tell stories about the dancers and the court, as her grandmother had done when Malila was small.

One evening as the wind drifted through the slatted windows and the insects sang a soft whirring song, Malila's grandmother said, "Malila, draw me a princess wearing a pink *pasin*. Make sure she has long hair and bangs."

Malila brought her chalks and tablet to her grandmother's side. As she sketched, her grandmother began to speak. Her voice was low and halting.

"The princess in the pink sarong is about to take a journey. She will take a sampan to Bangkok and then fly on a great silver hawk to America. She will leave Thailand because there is nothing there for her now. She is going to live with her mother."

Malila stopped drawing and looked at her grandmother. Her eyes filled with tears. The picture blurred in front of her.

Her grandmother seemed tired and she was now almost whispering. "The princess is sad to leave Thailand and all she has known, but Buddha will reward her *tam boon*. She will go to school in America. She will study art. She will use her opportunities to make her ancestors smile. She will have *sanouk*, the joy of living."

Malila lifted her chalk from the page. Grandmother covered Malila's hand with her own. "The princess will have *sanouk* because her grandmother wished it." She picked up the chalk that had fallen from Malila's fingers and placed it in Malila's hand. "Draw a grandmother in the picture, Malila. Draw her waving good-bye."

Malila began sketching again. As she drew, a tear dropped onto the princess's cheek.

Chapter Eleven~

THE FESTIVAL OF LOY KRATHONG was held during the full moon in November. Malila was leaving Thailand the next morning. Her suitcase stood by the door of the hut.

The night was crisp. Malila walked to the bank of the canal. As others had done, she placed a little cup made of banana leaves in the water. The cup carried a lighted candle, an incense stick, a coin, and a sprig of malila blossoms. The blossoms were mature, opened fully, snowy white and exuding a sweet fragrance. The release of a boat honored the water spirits and carried away the sender's sins. One also released a boat in honor of a dead relative. It was believed that if the fragile craft sailed away without snagging on reeds or capsizing, the soul of the loved one would have an easy journey to the next life.

Malila placed her hands in the *wai* and made the *krap*, the kneeling in respect for elders. She thought of her grandmother's soul, set free to join the souls of her ancestors. "May the dragon breathe on you no longer," Malila whispered.

Her little candle boat merged with the others and the twinkling lights drifted downstream. "Remember how it looks," she said to herself. "Remember how it sounds and how it smells. Take it with you, Malila. Remember it so that you never lose it."

She closed her eyes. Her mind drifted back to her childhood. She could see a little girl sitting on the floor next to an old woman who was sewing an elaborate costume. She could hear her grandmother's voice. "Malila, draw a red dress. A dress for the *fawn lep*.

"Malila, draw a blue dress of soft silk for dancing.

"Malila, draw . . .

"Malila . . ."

Malila opened her eyes and looked again at the river as it wound its way through the country, searching for its home. She watched as the current caught the little candle boats and sailed them downstream. The flames sparkled in the moonlight like diamonds.

Thai Words and Names

The Thai language is written in a different alphabet from English and contains sounds not found in English. It is a tonal language, with shades of meaning determined by the pitch of the speaker's voice rather than word stress. Pronunciations given here can only approximate the sound of spoken Thai.

bhiksu (pick soo): a monk

Chao Thi (chow tee): the spirit of personal protection, guardian of the home

chula (choo lah): a large kite used in kite fighting

ee tak (ee tock): a game played with a paper scoop and fruit seeds

farang (fuh rahng): a Westerner, a foreigner

fawn lep (fawn leb): literally "dance of the long nails," a traditional folk dance

haum (hom): literally "smells good," used as part of the names of food dishes to imply spiciness with a strong, pleasant aroma

jai yen (chai yen): literally "cool heart"; inner calm or personal peace

kao dom (cow tum): a sweetened rice dish

khwan (kwun): a spirit

klong (klawng): a canal

krap (krob): a very low bow, sometimes on the knees, made to show special respect for an elder, royalty, or a deity

krengjai (krayng chai): consideration and respect for other people

lakon nai (lah kawn nai): a theatrical dance, usually presented for royalty

Loy Krathong (loy krah tawng): a festival honoring the water spirits, celebrated in November

mai pen rai (my pen rye): never mind

malila noi (muh lee lah noy): a small flower that is purple when in bud and turns white when it opens; has a strong, sweet aroma

nam pla (nahm plah): a fish sauce

pakpao (pock pow): a small kite used in kite fighting

pasin (pah sin): a sarong

pla dek (plah deck): strips of raw fish preserved or marinated in a spicy sauce

ramwong (rum wawng): a folk dance

san phra phum (sahn prah poom): literally "spirit house"; a small replica of a house, the home of the guardian spirit Chao Thi

sanouk (suh nook): the joy of living

sawatdee (suh wut dee): a greeting: hello or good day

sawatdee pimai (suh wut dee pee my): Happy New Year

soi (soy): a street or lane

Songkran (sung krahn): the New Year festival, celebrated in mid-April, in which offerings are brought to the temples; one of the water festivals

suay (soo ay): unlucky

takraw (tuh kraw): a game using a rattan ball, usually played by children

tam boon (tahm boon): a sacrifice

Taowetsuwan (toe way tsoo wahn): a legendary giant

Tod Kathin (tawd kuh tin): a festival that marks the end of the rainy season

wai (wye): the action of putting the palms together to show respect; often used when greeting another person

wat (wut): the buildings of a Buddhist religious community–the temple and related offices

Acknowledgments

No one writes a book alone. Trite but true. There are many people I wish to thank:

Jimmy Buffett. I've never met the man, but his song "Changing Channels" convinced me to change mine.

Dinah Stevenson and her assistant, Miya Kanzaki. They took a pile of words and made a book. Thank you for my chance.

Mali Kennedy, who gave me her name to use in my book. Thanks for the loan, kiddo.

Susan Holesovsky, who read the first draft and liked it. Thank you for the encouragement.

Phillip and Sharon Holesovsky. Phillip helped me with the Thai language and told me about *suay*. They both sent me a Thai spirit house. Now the Chao Thi can protect me. Thanks.

Angelo Orsini, my grandfather, who reminds me eerily of Grandmother–wise and witty, a loving spirit. The dragon wouldn't dare breathe on him.

Jim Giles, husband, friend, critic, and mentor, who taught me how to walk among tigers. More than I hoped for.

Josh Jakubik, son, friend, all-around great guy. Thanks for being my kid.

To all my friends and family who believed in me and were happy at my good fortune. Thanks.

GAIL GILES is a BOI (Born On the Island) native of Galveston, Texas. She has an M.A. in Reading from the University of Houston and has taught reading and creative writing. *Breath of the Dragon* was inspired by the life story of a Thai student in one of her classes. The recipient of several literary awards, Ms. Giles makes her publishing debut with this book. She lives in Chicago with her husband, Jim, and three cats, Hemingway, Buffett, and Cujo. She has a son, Josh.

JUNE OTANI is a graduate of the Art Center College of Design, Pasadena, California. She has worked as an assistant art director in advertising, as a printmaker, and as an illustrator for fashion, decorative illustration, and children's books. For Clarion she illustrated *Chibi*, by Barbara Brenner and Julia Takaya. Ms. Otani lives in Hastings-on-Hudson, New York.

DATE DUE			